That's what you get...!

To Amy,

This is

Have fun!

Ric Walton

First Edition
05 04 03 02 01 00   5 4 3 2 1

Book published by
Gibbs Smith, Publisher
P.O. Box 667
Layton, Utah 84041

Orders: (1-800) 748-5439
website: www.gibbs-smith.com

Edited by Suzanne Taylor
Designed and produced by
Julie E. Gassaway of 1>10 Creative House
Website: www.onegreaterthanten.com

Printed and bound in Hong Kong

Library of Congress Cataloging-in-Publication Data

Walton, Rick.
   That's what you get! / text by Rick Walton; illustrations by Jimmy Holder.—1st ed.
      p. cm.
   Summary: A zany mother's rhyming explanations for why things happen.
   ISBN: 0-87905-964-8
      [1. Mothers—Fiction. 2. Humorous stories. 3. Stories in rhyme.] I. Title: That is what
you get!. II. Holder, Jimmy, ill. III.Title.

PZ8.3.W199 Th2000
[E]—dc21
                                                            00-023762

That's what you get...!

Rick Walton

illustrations by
Jimmy Holder

salt lake city

To Alan, Patrick, Nicholas, and Sarah Walton.
This is what you get.
R.W.

To Suzanne, my biggest fan.
J.H.

yesterday when I jumped from bed, I fell hard and bumped my head.

I told mom. she said, "Dear me."

"That's what you get for sleeping in a tree."

(Tonight try sleeping on a lower branch.)

yesterday when I washed my hair,
Bees attacked from everywhere.
I told mom. she said, "you're funny."

"That's what you get for washing with honey."

(Try vinegar next time. That will keep the bees away.)

"That's what you get
for brushing with glue."

(And speak up, dear. I can
hardly understand you.)

yesterday when I cleaned my room,
I kept tripping over the broom.

I told mom. she
thought a heap.

"That's what you get for dancing while you sweep."

(Next time just sing, dear.)

yesterday when I mowed the lawn,
I saw that all the grass was gone.
I told mom. she's really neat.

"That's what you get
for mowing the street."

(Now water the sidewalk, would you?)

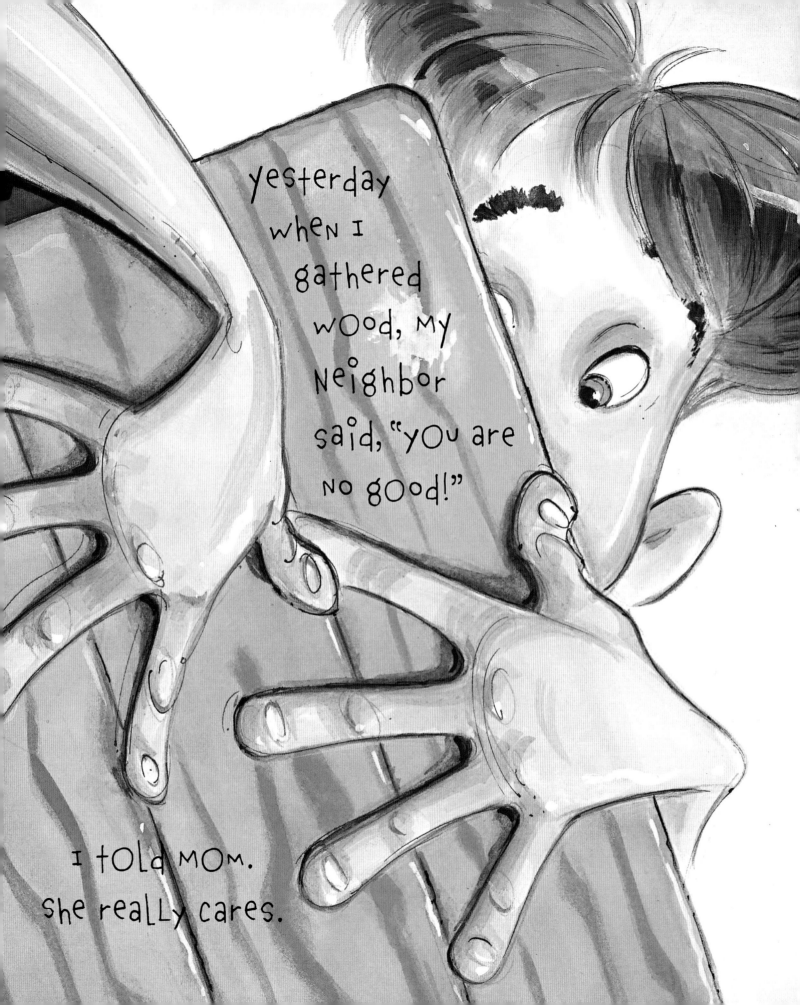

"That's what you get
for taking their chairs."

(And while they were sitting in them, too!)

yesterday when I tried to cook,
my friends gave me a funny look.
I told mom. She heard my news.

"That's what you get for cooking your shoes."

(I suppose you were making a filet of SOLE?)

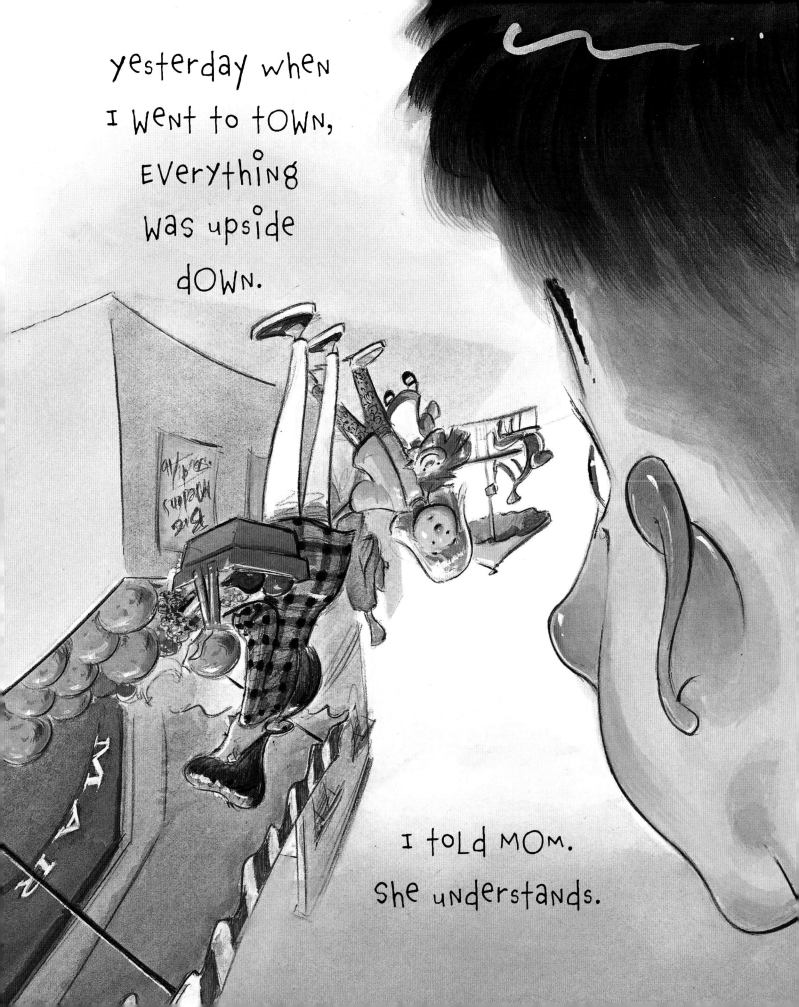

"That's what you get for walking on your hands!"

(But it does keep your shoes looking nice.)

"That's what you get for reading on the bus."

(May I borrow that book when you're done?)

yesterday when I tried to dance,
I fell down and ripped my pants.
I told mom. she has good sense.

"That's what you get for dancing on the fence."

(At least this time you weren't dancing with the broom.)

yesterday when I told a joke,
No one laughed. No one spoke.
I told Mom. She said, "Oh, please."

"That's what you get for talking to trees."

(And during their nap time!)

yesterday when I played my drum,
our neighbors criticized me some.
I told mom. she said, "Not bright."

"That's what you get
for playing at night."

(And under their windows, no less!)

Then today
when I looked
at you,
you were
good-looking

And smart
And strong
And happy
And graceful
And healthy
And talented
And really
wise, too.

I told Mom.
She took a look.

"That's what they get
for reading this book!"